The Garden Game

T0337798

Written by Julie Penn

Illustrated by Valentina Pieralli

Collins

Who and what is in this story?

Listen and say

Mum

bugs

Download the audio at www.collins.co.uk/839722

Dina

Ali

🎧 Dina and Ali are playing
a garden game.
Can they find the bugs?

Dina can see a bug. It's a red and yellow butterfly.

Look!

Dina can't see the bug now.
Where is it?

Ali can see a bug. It's a grasshopper. It's got big eyes.

8

Oh dear! This bug can jump.
Ali can't see it now.

Here's a bug. It's got eight legs.

Look!
It's a spider.

10

The spider can run!
Dina can't see it now.

Oh dear! The snail is going.
Where is it now?

Dina can see a bug.

Mum stops the children.

No! It's a bee.

15

Dina has got her camera. They are taking photos of the bugs.

There's a bug on the flower.
There's a bug behind the box.

There's a spider under the table.

There's a snail between the window and the door.

Dina and Ali count the bugs.

Picture dictionary

Listen and repeat

bee

bugs

butterfly

grasshopper

snail

spider

1 Look and order the story

2 Listen and say

Collins

Published by Collins
An imprint of HarperCollins*Publishers*
Westerhill Road
Bishopbriggs
Glasgow
G64 2QT

HarperCollins *Publishers*
Macken House,
39/40 Mayor Street Upper,
Dublin 1
D01 C9W8
Ireland

William Collins' dream of knowledge for all began with the publication of his first book in 1819.

A self-educated mill worker, he not only enriched millions of lives, but also founded a flourishing publishing house. Today, staying true to this spirit, Collins books are packed with inspiration, innovation and practical expertise. They place you at the centre of a world of possibility and give you exactly what you need to explore it.

© HarperCollins*Publishers* Limited 2020

10 9 8 7 6 5 4 3 2 1

ISBN 978-0-00-839722-7

Collins® and COBUILD® are registered trademarks of HarperCollins*Publishers* Limited

www.collins.co.uk/elt

British Library Cataloguing in Publication Data

A catalogue record for this publication is available from the British Library.

Author: Julie Penn
Illustrator: Valentina Pieralli (Beehive)
Series editor: Rebecca Adlard
Publishing manager: Lisa Todd
Product managers: Jennifer Hall and Caroline Green
In-house editor: Alma Puts Keren
Project manager: Emily Hooton
Editor: Emma Wilkinson
Proofreaders: Natalie Murray and Michael Lamb
Cover designer: Kevin Robbins
Typesetter: 2Hoots Publishing Services Ltd
Audio produced by id audio, London
Reading guide author: Emma Wilkinson
Production controller: Rachel Weaver
Printed and bound by: Pureprint, UK

MIX
Paper | Supporting
responsible forestry
FSC
www.fsc.org
FSC™ C007454

This book contains FSC™ certified paper and other controlled sources to ensure responsible forest management.

For more information visit: www.harpercollins.co.uk/green

Download the audio for this book and a reading guide for parents and teachers at www.collins.co.uk/839722